Creative Crown Turn That Frown Upside Down!
I Love My Natural Hair

This book is dedicated to the creative beauty of natural Black hair around the world.

and

The CROWN Act Led by The Crown Coalition

"Hi Nia, why is your face so stormy?" asked Grandma Sankofa. "My school day was not good. Why does Broderick giggle and stare at my hair?" Nia asked Grandma Sankofa.

"Well, maybe the giggles and stares
from Broderick are because
he doesn't know about your
Black Girl Magic!" said Grandma Sankofa
as she consoled Nia.

Grandma Sankofa said, "Nia, I'm sorry you have to experience this with Broderick. I will talk to your teacher Ms. Alice, about it. I am sure Ms. Alice will find a way to fix this. In the meantime, I want to show you some **royal bliss!**"

"Creative Crown, turn that frown upside down!" said Grandma Sankofa as she placed Nia's crown on her head. **"Look at me! I look like the Princess on TV!"** Nia said as she smiled.

"Creative Crown, turn that
frown upside down!"
said Grandma Sankofa.
**"Look at me! Click clack,
my beads look like my afternoon snack,"**
giggled Nia.

"Creative Crown, turn that frown upside down!"
said Grandma Sankofa as she adjusted Nia's crown.
"Look at me! One, Two...I love my afro puffs!
Yes... I am more than enough," said Nia with confidence.

"Creative Crown, turn that frown upside down!"
said Grandma Sankofa as sparkles filled the room.
**"Look at me! Look at my braids with strings of gold,
I am Brilliant, I am Beautiful, I am Bold!"** said Nia.

"Creative Crown, turn that frown upside down!"
said Grandma Sankofa. "Look at me!
Look at my rainbow of barrettes,
that's the day I played my
clarinet!" Nia exclaimed.

"Creative Crown, turn that
frown upside down!" said Grandma Sankofa.
"Look at me! Look at my pretty head wrap,
I look like my aunt Kelese,
she travels the world spreading peace."
Nia explained.

"Creative crown, turn that frown
upside down!" said Grandma Sankofa
as she made sure Nia's crown was just right.
"Look at me! Look at my ponytails and baby hair,
they make a perfect pair," said Nia.

"Creative Crown, turn that
frown upside down!"
Grandma Sankofa sang. **"Look at me!**
Look at my locs, my tips are dipped in red!
My hair looks like my daddy's flower bed," Nia said
as she smiled at her reflection in the mirror.

"Creative Crown turn that
frown upside down!" said Grandma Sankofa
as she reached to place Nia's crown on her head.
"Look at me! Look at my cornrows
and my colorful bow. Yes, that's me,
I'm all ready to go!" Nia said
as she touched her cornrows.

"Creative Crown, turn that frown upside down!
said Grandma Sankofa.
"Look at me! Look at my big curly afro.
Wow...it still has room to grow!"
Nia said as she admired her afro.

3ft

1ft

"Grandma Sankofa!
Thank you for reminding me
about my Creative Crown!
I will never walk around with a frown. Instead,
I will smile with glee, because
I am Empowered To Be Me!" Nia said
as she hugged Grandma Sankofa.

Sankofa is a Ghanaian word that means look back to move forward.
As I reflect on my childhood, I am reminded that my
natural hair was a significant part of developing my self-identity
as a young Black girl. The process of "getting my hair done"
was culturally affirming social emotional learning in action.
I was so proud of the creative ways in which the women
in my life styled my hair, from the perfectly parted, carefully
braided cornrows, and ponytails, to the colorful, bows, beads,
barrettes, binder balls, and ribbons that adorned them.

I learned how to wait patiently while my relatives and neighbors
got their hair done. While waiting, I practiced mathematics as
I counted the beads and barrettes and organized them into
patterns of bright colors and different shapes and sizes.
I used my imagination to think about what creative hairstyles
would emerge for me, my friends, and relatives.
I also calculated how long our hairstyles would last before
we got our hair done again.

Amazingly, as I look back, I remember the hair that naturally grew out of my head was my first experience with artistic expression, my hair creatively reflected my personality. The sacredness of sculpting and weaving natural hair into a piece of art is a beautiful experience. It felt so magical to go from one hairstyle to another.

More importantly, we unknowingly practiced the African traditions of socializing and relationship building as we had sacred time with the women who braided our hair. Passing down wisdom about family, community, culture, values, strengths, school, gifts, talents and more. It was also a time to engage with other girls that looked like me, we admired and complimented one another's hair as we shared the beautiful lived experience of "getting our hair done."

With Natural Hair Love,
~Dr. Talaya L. Tolefree

Made in the USA
Middletown, DE
28 September 2022